BREAKING
THE
CURSE

BREAKING THE CURSE

BOOK 1

Family Secrets

DR. LEXY DAVIS

This book is a work of fiction. The names, characters, dialogue, incident, companies and organizations, and places, except for incidental references to public figures, actors, places, products, or services, are the producer of the author's imagination and are not to be construed or depicted as real. No character of this book is an actual person and any resemblance to actual events, persons living or dead, or locales is entirely incidental. The author has made every effort to ensure the accuracy and completeness of the information provided in this book and assume no responsibility for any errors, inaccuracies, inconsistencies, or omissions contained in this book.

Cover design created by the author and illustrated by Digital_Quaslm

First Edition of Book I: February 2021

Printed in the United States of America

ISBN: 978-1-7365755-9-8

DEDICATION

This labor of love is dedicated to the memory of my beloved grandmother, Dr. Reverend Mattie Burruss and mother, Victoria Lorraine Enoex.

CONTENTS

FORWARD

*B*reaking *The Curse* is that most unusual of contemporary novels: a book steeped in truth, but with the storytelling power of great fiction. The book presents in realistic detail a problem that faces all contemporary minorities: how do we keep up the façade of success? At what cost?

We are far removed from the days of Fannie Hurst and Olive Higgins Prouty, who were able to couch their social criticism in a wash of melodrama that, in its own way, often undermined the very potent themes. There is no space today for Stella Dallas peering in at her daughter's wedding from the street, an outcast because she was a "fallen angel." Nor is it the time for Charlotte Vale to get over her insecurities by "saving" the daughter of her errant boyfriend. Today's fiction requires grappling with situations that have improved... but remain frustratingly problematic, nonetheless.

Nor is the book like Terry McMillan's seminal novels such as Waiting to Exhale, which showed that Black women could suffer the same sort of upper middle-class tragedies as their white contemporaries, only with a bit more moxie and less self-oppression. It could even spawn an enormously successful film which for some reason did not start an entire string of life-affirming but emotionally resonant films that white performers now are "too cool" to perform.

What struck me most about the book is its clear-eyed

view of the real challenge of being an upwardly mobile member of a minority culture who has bought, perhaps too well, into the Hollywoodized view of what the American Dream SHOULD be about rather than what it is about (endless acquisitiveness as a means of isolating one's self from the stresses of the world rather than finding an emotional base not based on material consumption).

The main character, Charlie Knight, to outward appearances is the ultimate example of someone who has "arrived." Chic, self-possessed, having an haute bourgeois career as an attorney about to face her first class-action lawsuit case. She is everything that a role model starved little girl looks at and hopes to be some day. But Charlie has a secret... behind the nails, the perfect body, the designer outfits, the degrees, and all the bling one could want, there is something absent in her core.

What is that? A secret. A secret that dominates her entire family. A secret so bad that Charlie has one crucial choice: face it, deal with it, and move on – at the potential risk of shattering the illusion of "having arrived," or keep it buried. Keep up the façade. At the beginning, she has clearly chosen what she felt was the correct mode: bury it. If money cannot buy happiness, it can rent it, and she intends to rent it at ever increasing levels.

But the truth will come out. Charlie WILL have to face her demons. It is for this reason that the book is a worthy successor to the entire tradition of bestselling novels about self-actualization. It brings the story to communities that have been largely absented or made to conform to dominant culture narratives.

As an Asian who grew up in a world where the only requirement was to smile, ignore prejudice, work behind the scenes, and win through sheer will to power and delayed gratification, I came to know all too well the mantra that "it doesn't matter what happens inside the house as long as the neighbors remain jealous of how perfect your life is." I had thought that was an Asian-only issue. Dr. Lexy's book came as a shock to me because it underlined with a magic marker how this is a UNIVERSAL problem, not an ethnic one.

Dr. Lexy's *Breaking The Curse* short stories, then, cross over lines of class, culture, race, and gender. It speaks to that human need to get external approval even at the cost of internal strife. It proves that this quest is, in fact, a false security, and that only by accepting the dark truths can one move forward and finally confront the possibility of a true happiness; not one that exists merely because of the Gucci label.

Dan Watanabe, Cinema Television Instructor

CHAPTER 1

Courtroom Decorum

There she was, grabbing her food order and leaving the line at the food court in the airport, heading to her departure gate for Washington, DC. Always aware of her surroundings, Charlie Knight, Esq. doesn't realize she has caught the attention of travelers, especially a mother and her daughter. Sitting with her five year-old daughter in the food court, the mother leans over to her daughter to draw her attention to Charlie.

"You see that tall lady walking there with the gold blouse? Look at her confidence. She looks as if she has the world eating out of the palm of her hands!"

Determined to get through her family's devastating

secret, Charlie walked through the airport with the confidence and resiliency of an endangered Siberian tiger on the verge of catching its prey. That's Charlie. Always razor-sharp and laser-focused. If you see her in a fight with a bear, help the bear. But in this case, might she be the one who finally needs help? This family secret is certain to test every ounce of resiliency she has in her mind, body, and soul.

After years of hard work, Charlie was well on her way to defending her first class-action lawsuit before the Honorable Judge Howard Vanzetti. Vanzetti was known as a hard-ass Superior Court Judge and tough on newly-minted attorneys. He was also known to be fair if freshmen attorneys were respectful, showed an enhanced ability to clearly demonstrate an understand ing of courtroom protocol and decorum, and had a deep understanding of the law.

Vanzetti, an Italian-American, is the second oldest of 12 children born to Giovanni and Annabella Vanzetti of Italy, in a characteristic quaint village in Savoca, Sicily. Savoca, an impeccable old-fashioned town in eastern Sicily, is known for its tombs, scenic villages, and well-known places of worship.

A distinguished-looking man, Vanzetti has fascinating hazel-colored eyes that radiate like a laser piercing the hardest of surfaces. He's strikingly handsome for a man who is 68 years old, and sits upon his bench with purpose and superiority; dressed in a black robe with gold piping, and sporting gray-blondish hair that looks as if it was styled straight out of the 1980s era. Vanzetti was quite handsome, to say the least, with a 6'5" athletic build.

Vanzetti, father of six adult children, is a widower after 43 years of marriage to the late Giselle Cabonaro-Vanzetti. He had been a United States District Attorney for 25 years, before becoming a sitting Superior Court Judge for the last 11 years. Vanzetti spent his earlier days in the Department of Justice, prosecuting crimes against state and local laws.

During his days as a United States District Attorney, he had a wide range of discretion on whether to prosecute cases, what charges to file, or whether to permit his opponents to plead their cases. This class-action lawsuit would become Vanzetti's greatest courtroom litigation, sure to go down in history as the modern day battle between David and Goliath.

Charlie, is a 42-year-old partner in a private practice law firm. Her firm was hired to represent consumers who are respondents in a class-action lawsuit against a major pharmaceutical company in Los Angeles. Charlie was president of her law school the last two years in college, and made quite the reputation for herself in the legal realm while completing field work. Established herself as a laser-focused, up and coming attorney, which played a major part in securing this case for her firm.

As an important part of Charlie's research for the case, she needed to compile a dossier on the Honorable Howard Vanzetti. This would be her first time appearing before him and she wanted to learn everything she could about him, leaving no stone unturned. She couldn't help but ask herself whether there were any hidden parts of his life on his journey to becoming a Superior Court Judge. If anyone could find a needle in the haystack, it would be Charlie.

Charlie was known as a game-over kind of corporate attorney, and she was the epitome of courtroom decorum and execution. Watching her go up against opposing attorneys in the courtroom with grace, poise, and determination was like watching any of the greatest boxers annihilate his or her competitors to the point of unconsciousness, forcing them to throw in the white towel.

As such, her charisma would hypnotize you, sending you straight into an involuntarily-pleasing, daydreaming state of mind. Charlie's appearance was just as amazing as her intellect. She wore her micro-thin golden braids, tightly pulled back into a ponytail and wrapped around into a soft bun, justly slightly above the back of her head. She donned white pearl earrings and a single strand pearl necklace, a black Donna Karan pantsuit accented with a white blouse, and three-inch Michael Kors black pumps. Charlie's makeup was flawless and as natural as it could be. She was courtroom ready, and always maintained a delicate balance of charismatic and analytic charm.

Charlie is well-educated and measured, but tougher than a hundred-year-old tortoise shell. You would rather be interrogated by the FBI for 48 hours, without food or water, than go up against a special-piece-of-work like Charlie. There were countless numbers of opponents who never saw the proverbial cut coming, until they looked behind them and their limbs were on the ground. A meticulous cut that could only be executed by a trained butcher. Charlie was a sharp-shooter in the courtroom. Never missed her target.

Chapter 2
The Partners

Charlie needed to travel to Washington, D.C. on Monday and was hopeful to get her request granted by the judge to recess for 90 days to do more discovery. The thought of appearing before Vanzetti sent a momentary chill through her body, as if the cold air of a blizzard had suddenly blown straight through her body. She shivered for a moment, but then shrugged it off so she could stay focused.

The class-action lawsuit against Colonial Pharmaceuticals was bound to become one of the most visible cases for the firm; a huge undertaking to say the least. This case would be the equivalent to a modern-day

Trojan battle between Achilles and Hector. All bets were on, that Charlie and her partner would emerge as the victors. Her partner, Vincent Masters, had planned to leverage the services of another bad-ass law firm that had a winning streak against several health industry giants.

Vincent Masters, Esq. is 10 years older than Charlie, with a solid frame in appearance, and simply masterful in the courtroom. If Charlie is the sharp-shooter, Vincent would be the equivalent to a dragon-slayer. He took down so many companies in class-action lawsuits that many of them preferred to settle out of court than go up against his brilliant mind. Vincent and Charlie's courtroom takedowns preceded them. They sharpened one another.

A native of The Bronx in New York, Vincent worked in some of the most sought-after law firms in Southern California. In the early 1990s, Vincent decided to transition into a private practice. He had represented class-action lawsuits against some of the most prestigious corporations and caught Charlie's eye in her second year of law school. Prior to meeting Charlie, his most recent victim was the corporate giant, Tech World, which was a mega giant in the dot-com era. .

Charlie reached out to Vincent, requesting to complete

her field work in his law firm. Once Vincent laid eyes on Charlie, and as they began to take deeper dives into legalistic conversations, he was convinced that she needed to be on his team. Soon after Charlie completed her field work, Vincent wasted little to no time taking her under his wings. Charlie became his prodigy after passing the bar, and their professional union would become a legacy foretold many centuries from now. As legendary as Camelot.

Considerably healthy clients, represented by the Masters & Knight Law Firm, suddenly began to die. The common thread between each of them was that they were all recent consumers of a dietary supplement manufactured and sold by Colonial Pharmaceuticals. Purchased bottles of the dietary supplement was tested and found to have excessive levels of lead and other contaminants.

The multivitamin, Vatexin, was recalled six months ago, at which time Charlie and Vincent had secured some of the top lead poisoning and health specialists to interview their health-stricken clients. Needless to say, their client's medical costs for what seemed to be an incurable health issue were mounting up on a daily basis.

The law firm planned to leave nothing undiscovered,

which is why they needed a recess to compile solid evidence that would knock the pharmaceutical giant off its feet. Going up against Colonial Pharmaceuticals wasn't going to be an easy feat, and if Vincent and Charlie ever needed to dig deep to win a case, this would be the time to get out their shovels and start digging.

Charlie is making the case for a recess and it appears that the Honorable Vanzetti is transfixed on her.

Wow, she is as stunning as she is brilliant. If only I could spend some time with her, Vanzetti wished.

Once done addressing the court, Vanzetti honored Charlie's request for a 90-day recess and struck his gavel, symbolic of his sharply-defined action. The sound of the gavel vibrated loudly throughout the courtroom.

Charlie said, "Thank you, Your Honor!"

The defense didn't object because it also needed more time for discovery.

"This case is in recess until ninety days, which takes us to January 5th," said Vanzetti.

For Charlie, this day would be forever etched into her memory for more reasons than one.

It's Friday and Charlie is excited about traveling to Washington, D.C., especially hanging out with her childhood girlfriends. She's connecting with all the people she loves within the next couple of days, starting with standing Sunday night dinner plans with her husband and parents at their favorite restaurant in Redondo Beach.

After dinner, she plans to go back home and rest up for her early Monday morning flight to Washington, D.C., where the fun begins with her thicker-than-thieves childhood confidants. There are no friendships on earth like that of Charlie and her four girlfriends from childhood, who are affectionately known as Corporate Bellas (CBs). They are in sync with one another and tighter than a tongue frozen to a pole in a snow blizzard.

Charlie is contracted to deliver an important keynote address for one of the opening sessions at a prestigious signature event in D.C. Her life is finally coming together seamlessly, and all the sacrifices she's made are beginning to pay out dividends. At last, life is great for Charlie and her family!

CHAPTER 3

The Starrs

Charlie's parents are Dr. Langston and Reverend Victoria Starr, and she is their firstborn. Next in line are her sisters, Catherine Starr-Hayley and Francine Starr, then her brother, Langston Jr., who is the youngest sibling. Each of them has children, which make Langston and Victoria very proud grandparents. The Starrs have been married for 44 years and are celebrating their 45th wedding anniversary next year in March.

An ordained minister, Victoria just finished preparing an outline for her Wednesday Night Bible Study for next week at New Faith Baptist Church. She is a legacy preacher, following in the footsteps of her late mother, Dr.

Reverend Maxine Singleton. Dr. Singleton was one of the first female ordained ministers in the city of Los Angeles, and passed away several years ago. Victoria was appointed by the New Faith Baptist Church Board to resume senior pastoral duties and was revered by her entire church community and its members.

A non-traditional job for women, presiding over a congregation was historically occupied by men. Reverend Singleton laid the groundwork and path that her daughter has embraced. Victoria is a woman after God's heart and has made it her priority to balance her relationship with Him and spend quality time with her family.

It's 2:00 pm on Sunday afternoon and Victoria opened the door to her study to call out to Langston. Often, she had to remind him to get ready for their dinner plans, especially on Sundays. Every Sunday at 5:00 pm was special as they looked forward to their standing dinner with Charlie and Bradley at the Golden Garden Restaurant in Redondo Beach. Victoria and Langston were a distinguished-looking couple and turned many heads whenever they were together or apart.

Victoria, was 5'9" with a caramel skin tone, brown eyes, with light-brown and curly shoulder-length hair, infused with specks of gray. She was every bit as fascinating as the colors on an autumn day in the Redwood Forest. A woman in her 60s, Victoria had a silhouette that most women 30 years her junior could only hope to possess.

Langston stood 6'4" and closely resembled Billy Dee Williams. You know the fine brother that starred in the movie Lady Sings the Blues? Dr. Starr is a neurosurgeon with a private practice. Although they live in Pacifica Palisades, they continue to operate their respective businesses in the underserved communities where they both grew up.

Langston yelled out to Victoria, "I'm here in the family room! What time is it now?"

"It's just after two pm," Victoria shouted back.

They have this way about themselves when shouting out in their palatial home. They both lean their heads sideways into the shout as if they're trying to direct traffic by signaling with their heads first.

"Charlie and Bradley will meet us at the restaurant, so let's plan to leave here at four-thirty, instead," Victoria answered.

In the family room, Langston was also making use of some downtime to get ahead of a couple of scheduled surgeries on Tuesday morning.

"Sounds good to me. I need to finish charting some files, but I'll be ready!" Langston said.

"Okay, Dr. Starr," Victoria left her study and started heading up the stairs. "I'll be in the bedroom resting a bit," she replied as she disappeared into the bedroom.

As normal as their conversation sounded, they both were a bit unsettled about the family secret they felt compelled to reveal to Charlie at tonight's dinner. Maybe it was a bit intentional that they stayed in their respective spaces to keep their minds occupied. At least for the time being.

CHAPTER 4

The Secret

As Bradley and Charlie entered the restaurant slightly before 5:00 pm, the concierge greets them.

"Welcome back to the Golden Garden, Dr. and Mrs. Knight! I see you have your standing reservation for four, which tells me your parents will be joining you this evening."

Charlie answers, "Yes, they should be walking in any moment."

Before Charlie could finish her sentence, the door opened swiftly behind her, and in walked the Starrs.

"Did I hear someone talking about us?"

Charlie greets them and says, "Hey Dad, Mom, you're right on time!"

Being on time is a gene that Charlie definitely got from her mom. She gives her mom and dad a tight squeeze and kisses them both on the cheek.

Charlie is a daddy's girl and her mother's clone. Not only did the apple not fall far from the tree, but the apple was still hanging on the branch. Victoria had always been a protective momma bear with her four children, and would lay down her life to continue protecting them. However, tonight's conversation will certainly compete with Victoria's protectiveness over her children.

"Hey son!" Langston said to his son-in-law, Bradley.

A bit nervous, Bradley extended his response.

"Hey Dad, Mom! You both look great tonight!"

Now, why is he acting nervous and shifting? Charlie is thinking. *As a matter of fact, he's been a bit distant today and I only wished I took the time to speak with him to see if anything was going on with him.*

As usual, Charlie shrugged it off and returned her attention to the present.

Bradley was similar in stature to Langston, so much so that they could pass for twins. It was clear that Langston was an older version of Bradley. Charlie admired her father a great deal, as he has always been her hero and confidant. They could talk about anything and they did. So it's no surprise that she married Bradley as he reminded her of her father. Typical of what daughters do, right? Grow up and marry men who resemble their fathers. Well, at least, it's exactly what Charlie did.

The restaurant hostess escorted the Starrs and Knights to their usual table near the window, with a stunning panoramic view of the Pacific Ocean. The table was lit with pillar candles and a fresh bouquet of rainbow-colored roses. The ambiance in the restaurant was warm and elegantly filled with the aroma of tantalizing flavors that resembled garlic, butter, and smoked apple wood that would make anyone's taste buds salivate.

Bradley's thoughts were far off but Charlie knew that he always felt some kind of way when she planned a trip with her childhood girlfriends. Maybe that's why he'd appeared distant during the day. What Charlie couldn't figure out, is why her mom and dad were unusually quiet at the table. Those two were always chatting it up, causing everyone around them to laugh out loud because of their comedic timing. But tonight, they appeared a bit jittery.

Charlie's discernment was always spot-on, especially when it came to her parents.

They couldn't be having problems in their marriage, she thought. Dad would have told me something.

Charlie thought maybe her parents had a disagreement of some sort and so she chalked it up to be just that and nothing more. Her mom could be hoity-toity at times and her dad was also known to be stubborn, especially when he was tired.

Watching the two of them ebb and flow was like watching synchronized swimming in the Olympics. Their chemistry is a sight to behold. But something's off with everybody at the table tonight, Charlie thought.

Charlie didn't realize that the three of them were about to reveal something that would take flight in her mind and not land for quite some time. In just a short period of time, Charlie would experience the kind of plane turbulence that sends flight attendants scurrying for their seats as the captain says, "Sit down, now!"

Victoria had planned to take this long-hidden family secret to her grave, but her hand was forced and the clock had already started ticking. She wanted to do whatever damage control possible and talk to Charlie, before a stranger would reveal it to her instead. Someone gave her an ultimatum and Victoria didn't hesitate to agree to be the messenger.

In hopes of softening the landing, Victoria decided it was time to tell Charlie the truth. Yes, she thought about doing it in the privacy of their home, but Victoria also knew Charlie would never make a scene out in public. Charlie was always level-headed and able to talk through the most difficult of conversations.

Charlie was too classy and dignified and, no matter what the circumstance, Charlie was resilient enough to hold it together. And yes, Victoria raised Charlie to be resilient in the face of trauma and tragedy, but this secret here would cause the devil himself to fall onto his knees and beg God for forgiveness.

At last, the conversation got underway. After ordering their meals, Victoria began to direct the conversation to Charlie, explaining that she had something very difficult she needed to share with her. Victoria began by saying how much she loved Charlie and how she prayed for God's help in sharing this with her.

Charlie's entire body began to stiffen a bit and chills began to run through her body as her mother continued to speak. As the words kept pouring out of Victoria's mouth, Charlie's body began to shiver. Charlie forced herself to inhale deeply and measured her breath as she exhaled. After she exhaled, Charlie released a scream just above a whisper with a low guttural voice. With her top and bottom teeth still together, Charlie moved her lips and began to speak.

"The three of you knew this for how long and just decided to tell me this now? Really! Right before one of my most important trips in my life? How awful of you, Mom and Dad. You too, Bradley?"

Charlie was furious. She slid her wedding ring off, slammed it on the table, pushed past Bradley, and stood up in all of her fury. If looks could kill, their hearts would have stopped beating immediately and all the air would have escaped from their lungs. Her laser-focused eyes were cutting through their souls.

Charlie's entire body trembled with anger and disgust. She looked at her father, as she tilted her head, with tears streaming down her face.

Victoria said in a muffled voice, "Charlie, please sit down, sweetie, so we can talk through this!"

Charlie stood there for a second, but it seemed like an

eternity. She continued to gaze at her dad with a far-off stare, then to her mom, and on to her husband and back to her mom. Charlie held up her right hand and pointed a trembling index finger at them all, while covering her mouth with her left hand, as if to muffle any sound trying to involuntarily push past her lips.

The still and silence of her apparent anger were accompanied by the kind of power that made her lips quiver, along with her finger. Charlie tried very hard to curse each of them out with every filthy curse word she could think of. The thought of these words tore at her insides, and her lips began to quiver uncontrollably.

All she could think of was how could words like that ever leave her mother's mouth, enter her chest cavity, and nose dive into her heart. A "rock-your-world" kind of conversation for sure. In the midst of anger, disgust, contempt, and loneliness, Charlie was broken and at a very low point in her life. How could she ever forgive them and recover from this? Charlie immediately thought, who else knew about this family secret? Did her siblings know? What about her children?

Victoria's heart sank into her chest and she was visibly shaken as she fell back onto her seat in the booth.

Victoria's face fell into both of her hands. She prayed that she would never see this day come into fruition. On a countless number of days, Victoria would lay prostrate before God praying for a different outcome.

Langston looked at Charlie with sadden eyes and tried his best to hold back the tears, while motioning to Charlie to come and sit near him. In that moment, Bradley began to edge out of his seat to reach out and embrace his wife. Charlie stretched out both of her hands, as if to push him back away from her.

Oblivious that the restaurant patrons and wait staff were looking in her direction, Charlie wiped away the flood of tears from her eyes and face. She rushed out of the restaurant, leaving behind her husband, mom, and dad.

They sat at the table with tear-filled eyes and anguish on their faces, feeling a sudden sense of grief-stricken loss and a deeply felt sadness. Before Charlie was out of view, Bradley leaped up to go after her. Langston grabbed his arm and told him with a cracked voice,

"Give her some space, son, and let her cool off. She'll come around," Langston said. "Just wait and see."

CHAPTER 5
The Mailbox

It's 9:00 am on Monday and Charlie stayed the night at the Hyatt Airport. She checked out of her hotel room, placed her luggage in the trunk of the car, slipped her sun shades onto her eyes, and slid into the driver's seat. Resilient, she was. Charlie jetted out of the hotel driveway, heading down the road to the airport to catch her flight to D.C.

Only five minutes from the airport, she decided to make a pit stop at her P.O. Box to pick up her mail. Her eyes were puffy and red from crying all night, and her heart was broken into a million pieces. Yet, she knew she needed to integrate a new memory into her brain, so she wouldn't be held hostage to the trauma she experienced the night before.

Charlie understood that she was in for an uphill battle and refused to succumb to this untimely, hard-landing family secret. As soon as she turned on her phone, a call was coming through from Bradley. She looked at the name on her navigating screen with venom in her eyes and let the call go straight to voicemail.

Charlie placed a quick call to her son and daughter, Bradley, Jr. and Sage, who were both away in college. Bradley, Jr. is a freshman at Standsfield University, and Sage followed in her mother's footsteps by enrolling into American University of Law in D.C.

Bradley and Charlie always took one another to the airport whenever they traveled, but today was different. Bradley knew that Charlie wasn't about to let that happen. Especially under the circumstances from last night. He was the last person she would expect to hold back something from her with such a catastrophic impact.

Charlie was expecting for some test results to arrive at her P.O. Box and, since the post office is on the way to the airport, now was a good time to see if they had arrived. Driving her metallic gold convertible sports car, a graduation gift from her daddy, Charlie swerved into the post office parking lot. She pulled into a space slightly in front of the door entrance. She stepped out of the car in one graceful motion. No one would have ever known that her insides were shattered the night before.

Charlie stood up confidently with her 5'10" frame, with curves most women would kill for and men longed to caress. She wore 18-inch blonde micro-braids, swinging left to right to left as she walked. She entered the door with a sense of urgency as if she were rockin' the cat walk during Fashion Week in New York. Standing in front of the mailbox, Charlie removed her shades and hoped that the test results she had been waiting to arrive the last eight weeks were inside her mailbox.

Charlie looked downward towards her mailbox and kneeled down to the floor to open it. She was far-removed from the attention her tall silhouette commanded from onlookers. She got her sense of style from her grandmother. Before Maxine Singleton became a minister, she dabbled in the entertainment industry.

Charlie inherited many of her grandmother's passions, including singing and dressing. Every time she stepped outside, Charlie's ensemble was complete from hair to heels. She was born in heels. Today's outfit consisted of gold, strappy Calvin Klein three-inch heels and waist high boot-cut blue jeans, with a Donna Karan gold lamé fitted blouse.

As Charlie kneeled down to the floor, her gold-laced Victoria's Secret cheekinis were slightly exposed. Both male and female onlookers' eyes were fixated on her. Again, Charlie had a way of rendering people into a hypnotic state of mind.

Charlie opened her mailbox, stuck her hand inside to retrieve the mail, and quickly rummaged through it as if she were looking for a winning lottery ticket. She dropped all but one piece of mail to the ground with a simultaneous gasp. She clutched the envelope close to her chest and stood up and turned to lean again the wall.

"Great, it's here," she said.

Charlie stuck it in her purse and quickly scraped up the other mail from the ground, and rushed out of the post office. She hopped into the car and sped off to the airport to board her 10:45 am flight.

At the airport, Charlie pulled up to the no parking zone in the departure area, put the car in park, got her luggage from the trunk, and left the keys in the car. So furious at her dad, the car he bought her was the last thing on her mind. Charlie hurried into the building to check her bags. She put her purse strap onto her right shoulder and headed over to the food court with the grace of a gazelle to get a bite to eat. Charlie's food was ready within minutes. She paid the cashier and, as she walked to her departure gate, it was time to board first class passengers. She boarded her flight to Washington, D.C.

ABOUT THE AUTHOR

Dr. Lexy Davis

About The Author Dr. Lexy Davis Dr. Lexy Davis is the pen name for creator, visionary, educator, Adriene Davis, E.D. With 20 years of experience mentoring women across generations, she has a passion for helping others navigate difficult challenges and situations. As a long-time journal-writer, she's always had a passion for wordsmithing. Her love of reading, writing, and her active imagination morphed into her trying her hand at fiction.

Dr. Lexy Davis is a mother of two adult children, one grandson, and is the second youngest of eight siblings; big families mean a busy life! When she's not occupied as a mom, grandma, or sister, she can be found writing—of course!—or generally enjoying her other passions. She's a fan of cooking, always mentors those in need, loves to sing, and always makes time to keep her body and mind fit! She hopes to inspire others to write their books and intends to be the catalyst for future authors breaking into the genre.

BOOKS IN BREAKING THE CURSE SHORT STORY SERIES

Dr. Adriene Davis writes under the name Dr. Lexy Davis. If you love drama and suspense fiction, be sure to keep a look out for the soon-to-be-released, *Breaking The Curse*, books in this series.

Breaking The Curse: Take Flight (Book 2)

Breaking The Curse: Call-Waiting (Book 3)

Breaking The Curse: The Divide (Book 4)

Breaking The Curse: Twice Broken (Book 5)

Breaking The Curse: The Settlement (Book 6)

Breaking The Curse: The Recused (Book 7)

Breaking The Curse: The Father's Side (Book 8)

Breaking The Curse: Bradley's Tale (Book 9)

Breaking The Curse: Binding Lies (Book 10)

ACKNOWLEDGEMENT

I am forever grateful to everyone who contributed to this body of work, and for inspiring me so much so that I found myself crossing the finish line on my first, fiction, written body of work. I want to first and foremost thank God for giving me the creative imagination to execute my vision for this 10-book series.

I am forever grateful to Dan Watanabe and Doris Driver for your constant support, expert lens, and the countless number of times you spent time giving me constructive feedback on this book. You are incredibly-talented and brilliant individuals, and I am truly appreciative of and for your friendship.

I am forever grateful to Dr. Gustavo Chamorro, Mrs. Maria Madrigal, Mrs. Marbella Ruiz, and Mrs. Lorena Ruiz for being my muse and sharing encouraging words that ignited a special fire inside me. You all have shown me such incredible grace and your gracious support has not gone unnoticed.

To Chaplain Euvonka Farabee. I am forever grateful to you, my dearest friend, for being present in every conversation and for always depositing into and praying over my life. You are the kind of priceless friend that every woman need in her village. You possess a sense of humility and loveliness that is far beyond a price, and you are forever-etched into my heart.

To Cheri Gouthier. I am forever grateful for the 30-plus years of friendship and being a great sister-friend and confidant. Your presence in my life is invaluable and I am truly appreciative of your kind and generous spirit. Thank you, most of all, for always believing in my talent and cheering me on.

To my adult children, Sophia J. Alexander and Clive H. Vaughan, Jr. Although you both are launched and no longer in the house, you continue to inspire me to never stop reaching for my dreams. My heart is full when you are full, and I thoroughly enjoy having the role of being your mom.

And finally, to my little Prince, Cayden Rae Vaughan, my first grandchild and grandson who brings complete joy and adventure to my life. I am certain you will inspire me to write a children's book one day soon.